Fitz is swimming around the reef with his mom.
"Look at all those fish swimming together!" he says. "I wish I had a group of friends like that."

"Why don't you make some friends, then?" his mom asks.

Fitz frowns, confused. "How do I do that?"

"Well, first you find some other fish, and then you ask them to be your friends," his mom tells him.

Fitz the Fish

Finds His Friends

By Dakotah Pike

Copyright © Dakotah Gumm, 2022
First paperback edition August 2022

ISBN 979-8-9860157-2-9 (Paperback)

Typeset using More Sugar, More Sugar Thin, and Alice
Illustrated digitally using Canva Pro

This book is dedicated to my godchildren.
Tia Kotah loves you!

3

"Hm." Fitz thinks for a minute. "That sounds like a good idea. But where do I find them?"

"Look around," his mom says. "Friends can come from anywhere!"

4

Fitz swims off to find friends as his mom watches.
The first thing he sees is an anemone, a pink thing that he knows not to touch. Anemones can sting!

"Friends can come from anywhere," he says, "but not from an anemone!" Something orange swims out from the anemone. It's a fish, with stripes like his!

"Are you okay?" Fitz asks. "You should be careful! Anemones can sting fish." "Not me!" The fish rubs against the anemone. "My name is Catie. I'm a clownfish. Anemones can't sting clownfish."

7

Fitz is confused. "Why not?"
"Our bodies make mucus, or slime, that keeps the anemone from stinging us," Catie says.

"The anemone keeps us safe from things that might hurt us."

"Oh," says Fitz. "Well, I won't hurt you! My name is Fitz. Do you want to be my friend?"

"Yes!" says Catie. "Let's play Hide and Seek."

9

Fitz closes his eyes. "I'll count. You go hide!"

1... 2... 3... 4... 5... 6... 7... 8...

"Ready or not, here I come!"
Fitz opens his eyes. Catie is nowhere
to be seen. Where could she be?
He sees a pair of eyes poking out
from the rocks. There she is!

9...
10!

11

"I found you!" Fitz says.
"You found me?" Something gray swims out from the rocks and turns pink.
"You just changed colors! Who are you?" Fitz asks.

"My name is Olivia," she says. "I thought you were my friend Catie hiding in the rocks," Fitz says. "It's really neat that you can change colors."

14

Olivia turns purple. "I'm an octopus. I change colors to hide from predators."
"It's good to stay safe." Fitz says. "Do you want to play hide and seek with Catie and me?"
"Sure," says Olivia. "I'll hide while you look for Catie."

Up ahead, Fitz sees some seaweed moving. It must be Catie! "There you are!" he says, swimming closer.

The seaweed swims toward him.
"Were you looking for me?" it asks.
"Oh, sorry!" Fitz says. "I thought you
were my friend."
"I can be your friend! I'm Daniel."

"You have some seaweed stuck on you, Daniel," Fitz says.
Daniel laughs. "No, I don't. I'm a leafy seadragon. We look like seaweed to help us hide from things that could hurt us."

"Friends can come from anywhere, but I didn't know a friend could look like seaweed!" Fitz says. "I'm playing Hide and Seek. Do you want to help me find my friends Catie and Olivia?"

"That sounds like fun," Daniel says.
"What do they look like?"
"Olivia is an octopus that can change colors, and Catie is an orange and white clownfish."

21

"I see something down in the sand!"
Daniel says. "Maybe that's them."
Fitz looks down to see several small
creatures. "That's not Catie and
Olivia, but let's say hi! My mom says
friends can come from anywhere."

The green creatures sink down into the sand as Fitz and Daniel swim closer.

"Hi!" says Fitz. "I'm Fitz the fish, and this is Daniel the leafy seadragon. We're looking for our friends."

Slowly, the creatures peek out of the sand. "I'm Elsie, and these are my brothers Eric, Eddie, and Ernie. We're garden eels."

"Are you playing hide and seek?" Fitz asks. "The sand is a really good hiding spot."

"No," Elsie says. "We live in holes in the sand to hide from danger."
"Friends can come from anywhere!" Fitz says. "Even from holes in the sand."
"Do you want to play with us?" Daniel asks.

"That sounds like fun!" Elsie says. "Maybe we can play Tag after you find your other friends." "Yes!" Fitz looks around for Catie and Olivia.

He sees some familiar eyes in the seaweed nearby. It's Olivia! "Found you!" Fitz says.

"Good job!" Olivia says, swimming up and turning pink. "Did you find Catie yet?"

"Not yet," Fitz tells her. Then he spots something orange and white behind some rocks. "There she is!"

"Oh, you found me!" Catie says.

Fitz and his friends play together until his mom calls his name. "It's time to go home, Fitz!" she says. "It was fun playing with you," he tells his new friends. "See you later!"

29

"Did you have fun today?" his mom asks as they swim home.

"Yes!" Fitz tells her. "I made lots of friends. You were right. Friends can come from anywhere! I can't wait to play with them again."

The End

Definitions

<u>Anemone</u>: an underwater animal with stinging tentacles and a column-shaped body.

<u>Clownfish</u>: a fish with orange or black and white stripes. Clownfish live in anemones and are protected from the anemone by mucus.

<u>Garden Eel</u>: a long, skinny fish that lives in holes in the sea floor

More Definitions

<u>Leafy seadragon</u>: a small fish like a seahorse that looks like seaweed

<u>Mucus</u>: slime

<u>Octopus</u>: an underwater animal with eight arms, a soft body, and no skeleton

<u>Predator</u>: an animal that hunts and eats other animals

More by Dakotah Pike

The ocean is a scary place for a tiny fish, but ocean animals can be fun to learn about! Join Fitz the fish as he explores the ocean floor and learns to face his fears!

Visit <u>dakotahpike.com</u> for free printables and updates on future books.

About the Author

Dakotah Pike is married and has two beautiful children. She lives in Springfield, MO, and when she's not busy homeschooling her kids or writing new books, she can be found singing Disney songs at the top of her lungs. Follow her on Instagram and Facebook, @dakotah.pike.author

CPSIA information can be obtained
at www.ICGtesting.com
Printed in the USA
LVHW070844210722
723997LV00015B/422